Man in the Flying Lawn Chair

by
Caroline Cromelin,
Eric Nightengale
Monica Read
Kimberly Reiss
Troy W. Taber
and
Toby Wherry

A SAMUEL FRENCH ACTING EDITION

SAMUEL FRENCH

FOUNDED 1830

New York Hollywood London Toronto

SAMUELFRENCH.COM

IMPORTANT BILLING AND CREDIT REQUIREMENTS

All producers of MAN IN THE FLYING LAWN CHAIR *must* give credit to the Author of the Play in all programs distributed in connection with performances of the Play and in all instances in which the title of the Play appears for purposes of advertising, publicizing or otherwise exploiting the Play and/or a production. The name of the Author *must* appear on a separate line on which no other name appears, immediately following the title, and *must* appear in size of type not less than fifty percent the size of the title type.

MAN IN THE FLYING LAWN CHAIR

was originally produced in July 2000 at the 78th Street Theatre Lab in New York City: Mark Zeller and Dana Zeller-Alexis, Producing Directors; Eric Nightengale, Artistic director; Ruth Nightengale, General Manager.

It was directed by Eric Nightengale with the following cast:

LARRY	Toby Wherry
CAROL, ensemble	Kimberly Reiss
TOM, ensemble	Troy W. Taber
LUPE, ensemble	Monica Read
MOM, ensemble	Carey Cromelin

During the initial development process, Alison Mattera performed an invaluable service by documenting and arranging improvised scenes into text.

SETTING

Larry Walters' workshop and at various locations in West Hollywood and Manhattan.

TIME

Between 1982 and 1993

AUTHORS' INTRODUCTION

Man in the Flying Lawn Chair is the result of a series of rehearsal improvisations and workshops at the 78th Street Theatre Lab focusing on the life of Larry Walters, who, in 1982, ascended to 16,000 feet in a Sears & Roebuck aluminum lawn chair attached to forty-five surplus weather balloons. Ten years later, Mr. Walters hiked into the California mountains, pitched a tent, folded his clothes neatly and shot himself through the heart.

This ensemble-created piece was developed in the tradition of the Living Newspaper, where theatrical inspiration is drawn from people and events pulled from the front pages of newspapers and other media. Eric Nightengale, Artistic Director of the Lab, conceived of the idea after stumbling upon the story of Larry Walters in a magazine and, along with Toby Wherry, Caroline Cromelin, Kimberly Reiss, Troy W. Taber and Monica Read, began assembling a script.

In creating the piece, the actors drew material from research they had conducted and mixed it with whatever happened to be lying around the rehearsal room and their own imagination to arrive at an improvised scene. This work was documented and revised over a period of two years.

During this process, we used the story of Larry Walters and the facts behind his extraordinary flight as a launching pad to investigate what might drive a man to dream about embarking upon such a spectacular and foolish plan. Our intention was never to present a documentary of Mr. Walters' life, but rather to investigate obsession, fame, and the consequences of actually doing that one cool thing that you dreamed about doing when you were twelve years old.

In the original New York production, this process of creation informed the acting style and look of the show, resulting in a world set halfway between a garage workshop and the mind of Larry Walters.

Scene 1

(LARRY is discovered at a worktable, which is always present. He is working on a model. In a voiceover, two jocular hosts of a radio call-in show read a letter, accompanied by their laughter and raucous interjections.)

VOICEOVERS.
Dear Tom and Ray

I listen to your show every Monday at work. I love your show. My husband gets *Flying Magazine* and showed me this story.

Thought you both would get a boost from this.

Val Stalions
Saint Marks, Florida
Tallyho

You've heard of Rickenbacker and Lindbergh and Doolittle. You've heard of Yeager. But have you heard of Larry Walters? Probably not. Yet Walters—was made of that special stuff that separates aviation legends from the common run folk.

(Lights up on LARRY, sitting on a mountain ridge. By his side are a Bible and pistol. He picks up the Bible, looks through it and puts it down. LARRY serenely contemplates his surroundings as voiceover plays.)

In 1982, Walters, a truck driver by trade, bought a bunch of weather balloons at a surplus store. He filled them with helium and tied them to a lawn chair. He provided himself with a two-way radio, a parachute, some jugs of water and a rifle and then cut his conveyance loose from the bumper of his car, which was anchoring it to the ground.

Take a moment to imagine the thrill and terror of that ascent, transforming a man surrounded by the normal appurtenances of life— garden, house, sport-ute—into a speck floating in an infinite space. Had he rigged up some sort of seat belt? Did the chair tip and wobble? Did he call out to the antlike figures below: We don't know.

It is clear, however, that he violated FARs by passing through Los Angeles TCA without a transponder or a clearance. Two passing jetliners reported to controllers that they had seen a man with a gun seated in a desk chair at 11,000 feet. A helicopter went up to take a look.

(LARRY picks up gun, points it at his heart. Blackout. Sound of wind.)

CAROL. *(Voice in the distance.)* Larry, *come down*!

Scene 2

(LARRY and FANNY contemplate a lawn chair.)

FANNY. Summer models. I call her the Cadillac of lawn chairs. Pricey.

LARRY. It's a hundred and nine dollars.

FANNY. Yeah, ouch! Post-Labor Day Sale. She's got looks, strength, comfort. *(LARRY reaches for chair.)* Whoa, whoa, whoa, that's our display model. *(Two women shoppers enter.)* Welcome to Sears, ladies. Pretty, huh?

LARRY. That's a nice curve.

FANNY. Yeah, that's for looks.

LARRY. Look how flush that grommet is.

FANNY. Yeah, that's for strength. Yep. She's a state of the art. *(Women exit. LARRY sits.)* I'm just going to leave you two alone for a minute. My name's Fanny if you need anything.

LARRY. Fanny, I'm Larry. Larry Walters.

FANNY. Good to meet you, Larry.

(FANNY exits.)

LARRY. Fanny, Fanny, I need you to help me with something! *(FANNY enters.)* I need to do a tester.

FANNY. *(Calling offstage.)* Junior?

(JUNIOR enters.)

LARRY. *(To JUNIOR.)* Excuse me, my name is Larry Walters. I need you to stand right here with your hands like that. Fanny, you watch me. Just watch me. Just watch me.

(LARRY leans back in chair.)

FANNY. Whoa, whoa, whoa.

LARRY. You see that? Look at that.

FANNY. Yeah, but that's what she's supposed to do.

LARRY. That's a fifty-degree fold.

FANNY. Yeah, yeah but she's a collapsible lawn chair.

LARRY. That's an obtuse angle actually. *(To JUNIOR.)* Down, please.

FANNY. That's what she's built to do.

(JUNIOR exits.)

LARRY. That's very dangerous. What if that happens at … that's very hazardous.

FANNY. Fold her right up. Take her to the beach.

LARRY. You got spark welders? Cause I could spot weld it here, here—fix her right up.

FANNY. Perfect for the patio.

LARRY. No, the weld would add extra weight and that might throw her off ballast.

FANNY. Slides in the back of the wagon.

LARRY. What if I was to take my cordless, drill straight through this supporting aluminum brace, insert a three-quarter-inch graphite lag bolt, and then secure it on each end with two sauce flanges.

FANNY. Collapsibility. That's her main feature.

LARRY. Thank you, Fanny.

Scene 3

(LARRY sets up apparatus to weigh lawn chair. He attempts to balance the chair with a bucket full of Coca-Cola bottles. After finding the correct balance, he removes the bucket and weights himself holding it on a bathroom scale.)

LARRY. Larry plus bucket. Larry plus bucket equals one hundred and seventy-five pounds. *(Burps.)* One seventy-four point six.

CAROL. *(Enters holding a bag.)* Wow.

LARRY. Hi, Carol.

CAROL. Hi.

LARRY. Hi. Hello.

CAROL. Hi.

LARRY. Come on in, hello. Make yourself at home. Mi casa es su casa. My house is your house in Español. So what time's the movie?

CAROL. *Somewhere in Time* starts at 7:30.

LARRY. That's sooner than I thought.

CAROL. Well *ET* starts at 8:15?

LARRY. Oh no, I don't want to go all the way into Hollywood. Don't you want to see *Somewhere in Time*?

CAROL. Well I don't really know anything about it.

LARRY. Oh it's supposed to be terrific. It's got an all-star cast. It's got Christopher Plummer. Now don't get too excited, he has a very small part in this movie, but he's supposed to be terrific. And it's got Jane Seymour. And of course it's got Christopher Reeve. He's supposed to be amazing. He played Superman.

(Hums opening bars to Star Wars' *theme song.)*

CAROL. I think that's the *Star Wars* theme song though ....

LARRY. No that's Superman.

CAROL. *(Begins to hum theme song to* Rocky. *LARRY joins in.)* No, I'm pretty sure ... Larry, that's *Rocky*.

LARRY. *(Indicates bag in CAROL's hand.)* What's that?

CAROL. Oh, it's wine for dinner.

LARRY. Dinner?

CAROL. For the drive-in. The girl that I used to work with at Kroger's, she said it was good. Do you remember her?

LARRY. Uh, no I don't actually.

CAROL. She has lots of curly red hair, she's kinda big around the middle. Talks with a lisp.

LARRY. Dinner?

CAROL. Should I not have brought the wine?

LARRY. Oh, no, the wine's fine, it's just that I'm cooking chili, and I just don't know if wine goes with chili. I was thinking we could just drink Coca-Cola. Because people drink Coca-Cola with just about .... Things go better with Coca-Cola, things go better with Coke. You know what we could do? We could get chicken, chicken is a white meat and that is a white wine. Or we could get a fillet-o-fish sandwich.

CAROL. I don't know about a fillet-o-fish at the drive-in. They're very greasy.

LARRY. I just don't want you to be disappointed.

CAROL. Oh, no, I won't be disappointed. I'm not a picky eater.

LARRY. Now Carol, I'm known for my chili. When I was in Vietnam we had this one sergeant, "Have you guys tried Larry's chili?" "Oh yes sir, we've tried Larry's chili," from Ham Tam to Vo Dak to Dak Dam they all knew Larry's chili because I had a secret. You see, all these guys over there they would take these Thai seeds and they would crush them and smoke them. But I would take the Thai seeds, and I would crush them and I would put them in the chili.

CAROL. Is it really hot? Is that what you mean?

LARRY. Extremely.

CAROL. Oh.

LARRY. But if you take a mouth full of Coca-Cola and swish it around, it acts as a natural Novocain that counteracts and neutralizes the heat. And that is true.

(LARRY goes to his worktable.)

Scene 4

CAROL. Larry, Larry, just come inside. My mom's asleep.

LARRY. If only he hadn't looked at that penny.

CAROL. Or if they were naked they'd still be together right now.

MOM. *(Enters.)* Carol?

CAROL. Hi, Mom.

MOM. Hi, sweetie. Is Lar with you?

LARRY. Hi, Mrs. Van Duesen.

MOM. Hi, Lar, how was the movie?

CAROL. We saw *Somewhere in Time.*

MOM. Again?

CAROL. It was very romantic.

MOM. Oh Lar. Carol says the movie was very romantic. Did you find the movie very romantic?

LARRY. Very romantic.

(LARRY and CAROL kiss.)

MOM. Okay, kids. Okay. Good night.

(MOM exits.)

LARRY. Do you think that's possible?

CAROL. What?

LARRY. To do what Christopher Reeve's character did in *Somewhere in Time.* Just give up everything and travel back in time and risk losing everything for love.

CAROL. Well for the right person I know that I would.

LARRY. Do you think he died of starvation or a broken heart at the end of the movie?

CAROL. Can you actually die of a broken heart?

LARRY. I think it's more likely that he died from lack of water. The body can survive for a long period of time without food but only if it has a certain amount of water. That's why in the movie *Gandhi* they gave him water, otherwise he wouldn't have survived the movie. *(Doorbell.)* Carol, someone's at the back door.

MARIA. *(Enters.)* Hi, Larry.

LARRY. It's Maria De Guadeloupe.

CAROL. Hi, sweetie.

MARIA. Hi, Carol. Your cat coughed up a hairball on my dad's back porch today. What are you doing?

CAROL. It's late. What are *you* doing?

MARIA. Dad said Mrs. Van Duesen wanted to borrow his hammer.

CAROL. Okay, I'll give it to her. Tell your dad thanks.
MARIA. Okay.
CAROL. Okay.
MARIA. What's you guys doing?
CAROL. Go home, Maria.
MARIA. Okay, Carol. Bye, Larry.

(MARIA exits.)

CAROL. Are we really going to do this?
LARRY. We're going to do it right out there in your backyard.
CAROL. What happens when I can't see you anymore?
LARRY. I'm going to give you a walkie-talkie, and I'm going to have a CB radio and we're going to be in constant contact.
CAROL. How are you going to get down?
LARRY. I'm going to bring my gun.
CAROL. Oh.
LARRY. Imagine that I'm here and the balloons are here and I'm cruising at a maximum altitude of five hundred feet. Just above the houses. Now I want to come down. So I take my gun and I shoot out one of the balloons. And I come down like that. *(Begins making out with CAROL.)* I think I'm going to come down again. Oh I'm coming down very fast. You better notify LAX because I'm coming down between two unidentified flying objects. And now I'm coming into a valley.
MOM. *(Offstage.)* Here kitty, kitty. Pretty Girl?
LARRY. Meow. Meow.
MOM. Carol, sweetie, I can't find Pretty Girl.
CAROL. Mom, just look under the bed.
MOM. I can't look under the bed, Carol, I'm blind. Carol, I better come out there.
CAROL. No Mom, wait.
MOM. I think she might have gotten into the organ again.
CAROL. Mom, just wait.

(CAROL exits.)

MOM. Check the oven.

(During the make-out scene LARRY has tangled himself up in the chair.)

LARRY. Carol, I'm stuck.
MOM. She could have crawled into the Sanchez's barbecue pit.
LARRY. Carol, I'm stuck.
CAROL. Mom, she's not in the barbecue pit.
MOM. She's not here. She could be dead.
CAROL. She's not in the oven, Mom.
MOM. Please sweetie, check the oven door. She's not in here. Carol, she could be dead. Please check the oven, hon. She's not there, Carol Sweetie she's—
CAROL. She's under the—there she is. I told you.
MOM. Oh, there you are, you evil little thing. Sorry sweetie.
CAROL. That's okay.
MOM. Sorry for interrupting your date.
CAROL. Okay. Good night Mom.

(CAROL re-enters.)

MOM. Good night.

(After freeing himself from the chair, LARRY takes off his sneakers, anticipating more fun with CAROL, but he becomes preoccupied with suspending the sneakers by their laces.)

CAROL. What are you doing?
LARRY. Do you think I look like Christopher Reeve?
CAROL. You are way more rugged than Christopher Reeve.
LARRY. Carol?

CAROL. Yeah?
LARRY. I think that movie's going to affect an entire generation.
CAROL. Do you want to tuck me in? You gotta count to sixty.

(CAROL exits.)

LARRY. Sixty. Fifty-nine, fifty-eight ... *(Continues counting backwards during which time he takes a condom out of his pocket. He blows it up into a balloon, sticks it to the wall, places his lawn chair on the ground so that when he sits in it he is lying on the ground.)* Three, two, one.

(LARRY shoots the condom with his pistol.)

Scene 5

(Sound of truck backing up.)

LARRY. *(To driver in truck.)* Okay, bring her on back.
TOM. A lawn chair? Are you nuts?
LARRY. It's the Cadillac of lawn chairs. Hundred-percent aluminum with countersunk pop-riveted grommets. *(To truck.)* Sorry? I've been a truck driver for six years. I think I know—You're the one who wanted to drive!
TOM. Now wait a minute ... you're gonna what?
LARRY. Now cut it right there because you're getting close to the dock.
TOM. A lawn chair?
LARRY. Open-air flight, Tom. *(To truck.)* Stop! *(To TOM.)* No Spam in a can for Larry Walters.
TOM. Why don't you just go up in a hot-air balloon? Man, didn't

you ever see *The Wizard of Oz?*

LARRY. I spent two years in Vietnam working out the details of the loner module. And, yes, I did see *The Wizard of Oz* and that thing couldn't have lifted Toto.

TOM. You were in Nam? Where were you stationed?

LARRY. Over a pot of boiling potatoes. I was a cook. I cooked for a lot of kids who got killed.

TOM What kind of shoot is this anyway?

LARRY. It's a commercial shoot. That's all they tell us, that's all we need to know. We're truck drivers not directors. Hey, Tom, did you ever look at bubbles in boiling water? You can do a lot of thinking.

TOM. A lawn chair? Suspended by what?

LARRY. Balloon clusters.

TOM. Balloon clusters?

LARRY. It's a three-tiered system.

TOM. I don't get it.

LARRY. See, imagine I have a craft.

(LARRY sketches out a model.)

TOM. The lawn chair?

LARRY. Yes.

TOM. A lawn chair.

LARRY. Here's the loner module.

TOM. Larry?

LARRY. Now I have these lines that come off of it here …

TOM. Larry ….

LARRY. … and there and there and there.

TOM. What, do you wanna kill yourself?

LARRY. And they all converge right here on this one point.

TOM. Larry, you're crazy—first of all, you're gonna quadruple the weight of that lawn chair.

LARRY. Now this convergence point will hold all the weight of that lawn chair.

TOM. That's gonna take more rope than they've got around that ball of twine in Kansas.

LARRY. Really?

TOM. You would at least need to make a sling hitch and tie it off with a cat's paw. What's the distance between clusters?

LARRY. Forty feet.

TOM. That's almost half a football field.

LARRY. So I can't use a sling hitch and a cat's paw?

TOM. Yeah, but you need to put a thimble on the cat's paw. See there's two kinds of rope, Larry, static and dynamic. Dynamic is the springy stuff so if you're climbing and you fall you don't break your back, but if you tie a boat off with that it stretches right out and, "Sayonara, party barge." We better use static.

LARRY. Does it hold a knot?

TOM. Well, a knot is a closed nonintersecting curve that exists in three-dimensional space.

LARRY. Hey, Tom?

TOM. What?

LARRY. I thought that ball of twine was in Nebraska.

Scene 6

LARRY. Carol? You got the altimeter?

CAROL. Uh-huh.

LARRY. Carol?

CAROL. Oh, over.

LARRY. You got the CB radio?

CAROL. Check. And the parachute.

LARRY. You got the gun?

CAROL. Check.

LARRY. And you got the beef jerky and Coca-Cola?

CAROL. Check. Check. And the parachute.

LARRY. Carol, the Coca-Cola is very important because we're going to be up all night blowing up balloons.

CAROL. Wow! I know. It's going to be fun. Like a slumber party.

LARRY. No, it's more like NASA, really. We've got to get those helium tanks out of the front yard.

CAROL. Check.

MOM. *(Enters.)* Carol, where's Larry?

CAROL. Hi, Mom.

MOM. I need him to hang the Last Supper, sweetie.

LARRY. Oh, there's my hammer.

MOM. Mr. Sanchez's hammer, Lar.

LARRY. Carol, I need the hammer to hang the Fourth of July decorations ....

(A car honk.)

MOM. Carol, Larry, you should be careful of that ceiling fan, honey, it has blades.

LARRY. What's going on out here?

CAROL What's the matter?

LARRY. You should see all the cars in the alley.

MOM. Oh, Lar, Mr. Sanchez is having his annual Fourth of July party. You know all his relatives comes up to LA from Tijuana.

LARRY. But I told Tom just to shoot up La Cienga, and now he's going to have to come up the front.

MOM. Tom? Who's Tom, Lar?

CAROL. Mom, Tom and Larry work together. It's fine.

MOM. Carol, I can't have Tom coming over; my hair is a mess.

LARRY. Carol, it's not about the hair, it's about NASA.

CAROL. Mom, let's just make it a little party, okay?

MOM. Oh, a Fourth of July party.

CAROL. Yeah, that's a good idea.

MOM. *(Exiting.)* I have some sangria already made up.
LARRY. Less wine more fruit.
MOM. Oooo, Carol, I've got that bottle of grappa!
LARRY. No grappa!
MOM. … and I got some frozen nachos!
LARRY. Carol, she's going to turn on the oven ….
MOM. … I'm just going to heat up the oven ….
CAROL. Okay, I'm going right now. *(Exits.)* It's on.
LARRY. Okay. *(Doorbell.)* Carol, someone's at the front door.
CAROL. I got it. Check.

(CAROL exits.)

LARRY. Who makes sangria with grappa!
CAROL. *(Entering.)* Okay, it's on.
MOM. *(Enters.)* You're going to love this sangria, Carol, it's got mango and guava and strawberries—

(Doorbell.)

CAROL. *(To LARRY.)* I got it.

(CAROL exits.)

MOM. —and peaches and bananas and apples and orange and guava. It's wonderfully healthy! Where's my cuppie, sweetie, I need my cuppie, and pineapples and cherries and mango and guava and strawberries and peaches and bananas ….
CAROL. *(Re-enters with TOM.)* Here he is.
TOM. Hey, Larry.
LARRY. Hey, Tom. How ya doin', man?
TOM. What's happening, guy? Is this the machine?
LARRY. This is it. It's lacking a few parts ….
TOM. Did you get the flex-care 550 multi-weave?

LARRY. Yeah, it's in the back of the truck.

TOM. How long has it been back there? Didn't it rain last night? You know that stuff can deteriorate if exposed to moisture.

CAROL. Larry?

LARRY. That's why we're doing the fender drill—to make sure it's up to its rated load-bearing. If not, we'll just dry it.

CAROL. Larry?

TOM. Dry it? What, do you wanna put it in the oven?

MOM. The oven? Is someone lighting the oven?

LARRY. What?

CAROL. Introduce them!

LARRY. Oh. I'm sorry. Tom this is Carol's mom, Margaret Van Dueson. Tom, Margaret, Margaret, Tom.

MOM. I'm Margaret Van Dueson. I'm a little bit blind.

TOM. Pleased to meet you. I like the strawberry patch in the front yard.

MOM. You do?

TOM. My mom makes great shortcake—she uses these South Carolina berries, they're smaller but packed with flavor.

LARRY. Tom, you know Lindbergh carried strawberries on his trans-Atlantic flight.

MOM. Carol says the one's from Von's taste like cardboard.

LARRY. Preflight food prep is an important part of any mission, Tom.

MOM. Larry was supposed to put straw underneath them, so, you know, they don't get—

TOM. Fungus?

LARRY. But maybe more important is solid waste disposal—

MOM. That's why they're called "straw" berries, Lar.

LARRY. Captain Queeg.

MOM. Be careful, Tom, Larry's lactose … lactose …

LARRY. Intolerant. *(Doorbell.)* Carol, someone's at the back door.

MARIA. *(Enters.)* Hi, Larry.

LARRY. It's Marie De Guadeloupe.

CAROL. Hi, sweetie.
MARIA. Hi, Carol.
CAROL. What do you need?
MARIA. My dad needs some ice. We ran out of ice.
CAROL. Okay, hold that.

(CAROL exits.)

MOM. Hi, Lupe.
MARIA. Hi, Mrs. Van Dueson.
MOM. I heard the music next door.
MARIA. Yeah, we got a mariachi band. Wow, what's that?
LARRY. I'm hanging Fourth of July decorations from the ceiling fan.
MARIA. I don't see no stars and stripes.
LARRY. Carol!
CAROL. *(Enters.)* Maria, stop that.
MARIA. Looks like a high chair to me.
CAROL. Maria, stop that.
MOM. What, she's hanging off it? Lupe, be careful, you could get electrocuted, sweetie.
CAROL. Maria, you take this ice and bring it back to your father now!
MARIA. Okay, Carol. All right.
MOM. Lupe, be careful of the cats.

(MARIA exits. LARRY and TOM move to the lawn chair.)

LARRY. Tom, from this point on I'm going to need your undivided attention.
MOM. Oh, Carol—
LARRY. See, I'm going to need a pocket here for my beef jerky and Coca-Cola.
MOM. Tom sounds like a nice young man.
LARRY. ... the Coca-Cola is for caffeine.

MOM. Tom, do you like Ray Mancini?
LARRY. Henry Mancini.
CAROL. Mom, let me pick the music. Okay?

(CAROL turns on the radio.)

TOM. What do you think about these as attachments points?
LARRY. As long as it's secure. Here's where I want to put the altimeter.
CAROL. Hey, it's our song!

(LARRY and CAROL begin dancing. Doorbell.)

LARRY. Carol, someone's at the back door.
MARIA. *(Enters.)* Hi, Larry.
LARRY. Hola chica.
MARIA. Mrs. Van Dueson, my dad needs his hammer back.
MOM. Larry, sweetie, please, I need you to hang the Last Supper.
LARRY. Voulez-vous couches avec moi ce soir?
MOM. Larry, I didn't know you could speak Italian.

(MARIA goes to the chair, draped by a weather balloon.)

MARIA. Wow, what's that?
LARRY. It's a five-mil chloropyrene.
MARIA. Looks like a balloon.
LARRY. Well, it is a balloon. It's a weather balloon. It has a burst diameter of eight feet but that's only if you reach an altitude of twenty thousand .... *(MARIA picks up balloon.)* Maria! Maria!
MARIA. Smells like Barbie.
LARRY. Mayday! Mayday! Don't touch it! Tom, hands! Carol, balloon! Ignition!

(LARRY takes balloon from MARIA.)

CAROL. Maria!
MOM. Larry, honey, please I need you to hang ....
LARRY. Time out! Time out! Radio!
CAROL. Okay. Check.

(CAROL turns off radio.)

LARRY. I'm going to hang the Last Supper.
MOM. Thank you, sweetie. Lupe, I'm going to make you some virgin sangria.
MARIA. Okay.
CAROL. Larry, that's too high.
LARRY. She's blind.
CAROL. No, Maria, you can't drink that. You're just a little girl. You go take the ice and the hammer and bring it to your father right now.
MARIA. Okay, Carol. Bye, Larry.

(MARIA exits.)

MOM. Is it the vocal point, sweetie? Make sure it's the vocal point.
CAROL. Yeah. It is.
TOM. Why do you call it the Last Supper?
CAROL. It's a photo of the last Thanksgiving before Daddy ....
MOM. Tell him about the accident, sweetie, with the oven.
CAROL. No, Mom, no—we're not going to talk about the accident. I think you had a little too much sangria.
MOM. I think I had a little too much sangria.
CAROL. Okay, I think Mom's going to go to bed. Everybody say good night to Mom.
LARRY. Good night.
TOM. Good night.
MOM. Okay! Good night!

(MOM exits. Pause.)

CAROL. Okay, let's just do a tester.

LARRY. Okay, Carol, that's a good idea. We'll do a tester.

MOM. *(Offstage.)* Carol, sweetie, ask Larry to turn off the oven.

LARRY. I knew it, Carol. It's the picture, and then it's the accident, then the oven. Picture, accident, oven. She does it on purpose, Carol. She's giving me bad ju ju.

CAROL. It's off!

LARRY. I said she's giving me bad ju ju!

MOM. Is it off, sweetie?

CAROL. Yeah. It is.

(Pause.)

LARRY. I'm sorry, Tom. Carol, I'm sorry, I apologize.

(Pause.)

CAROL. You wanna suit up?

LARRY. Let's do a tester. All right? We'll do a tester. Let's just clear everything. Contact.

(LARRY begins to inflate weather balloon, using a canister vacuum cleaner. Doorbell.)

LARRY. Carol, someone's at the back door.

(Balloon continues to inflate throughout the rest of the scene.)

MARIA. *(Enters.)* Hi, Larry.

LARRY. What is she doing here?

CAROL. Maria, what are you doing?

MARIA. There are some cops outside poking around the front lawn.

LARRY. Cops?

LARRY, CAROL and TOM. The helium tanks!
LARRY. Routine six.
TOM. Tell them you're a dentist!
LARRY. That's a good idea.
CAROL. My mom has emphysema. They're her tanks!
LARRY. I like it!
TOM. Tell them we're scuba diving!
LARRY. No wait! Tell the cops we're doing a commercial shoot!

(CAROL exits.)

MARIA. Really? Can I be in it?
LARRY. Yes! Yes! Yes!
MARIA. Carol! I'm going to be in a commercial.

(MARIA exits.)

LARRY. *(Sings as balloon is still inflating.)* Oh, beautiful for spacious skies ....

(LARRY continues to sing through the end of America the Beautiful *as CAROL, MOM and MARIA enter.)*

MOM. *(Enters.)* Carol, honey, it's too late to vacuum.
MARIA. *(Enters.)* Whoa.

(LARRY finishes song.)

LARRY. Okay, Tom. *(The balloon now completely fills the room. TOM turns off vacuum.)* One down, forty-four to go.

Scene 7

LARRY. Okay, Tom, look out for that line. Have Carol help you.

CAROL. Larry, it's getting very tight around the fender of the car.

LARRY. It's getting close to the eave of the house.

MARIA. Larry, Larry I want to go up now.

LARRY. It feels like it's going to break.

MOM. Lar, Lar.

(At this point, the ensemble physicalizes a silent response to lawn chair take-off. Scene shifts.)

PILOT. Delta 1049, looking for LAX approach. We are currently at 16,000 and ready for descent.

AIR TRAFFIC CONTROLLER. Cop, Delta 1049, turn left heading 0-7-0, maintain 16,000 till establish localizer, cleared aisle S, runway 4, left approach.

PILOT. Aisle S, runway 4, left.

AIR TRAFFIC CONTROLLER. TWA 753, turn left, heading—

CO-PILOT. Joe, are you seeing what I am seeing?

AIR TRAFFIC CONTROLLER. 1-2-0, altimeter 29-er-9er2. Pan Am 2736, contact tower 1-18.3.

CO-PILOT. Delta 1049, level at 16,000 feet. We have a man in a chair attached to balloons in our 10 o'clock position, range 5 miles.

AIR TRAFFIC CONTROLLER. I've got something on my scope here without an ident.

PILOT. We are definitely seeing something up here. It looks like we've got a man with a gun in a chair.

AIR TRAFFIC CONTROLLER. Delta 1049, please repeat. You're saying there is a man with a gun on the plane?

PILOT. Negative, we have a man with a gun in what appears to be a lawn chair attached to what looks like balloon clusters, 5 miles off our 10 o'clock.

AIR TRAFFIC CONTROLLER. Delta 1049, are you claiming emergency status?

PILOT. That is a negative. This guy is a duck without a quack.

AIR TRAFFIC CONTROLLER. Delta 1049, descend and maintain to 5,000, follow the localizer, inbound speed 1-6-0, correction 1-8-0, immediately expedite.

PILOT. Immediately, roger.

(At this point, the ENSEMBLE breaks into dance or some physical expression that suggests the experience of flight. Scene shifts.)

CANDY. In some countries you have to like bag your own stuff.

SUSIE. You have to bag your own stuff at Von's.

CANDY. That's why they're like a local chain. You have to pick it out, put it in your cart …

SUSIE. What the heck is that?

CANDY. … put it in your cart and then like pay for it.

SUSIE. What the heck is that?

CANDY. People will do whatever they have to to get attention.

SUSIE. His little legs are like …

SUSIE and CANDY. … hanging.

CANDY. What's he doing now?

SUSIE. Well, I can't see him, just the balloons. The balloons are the only things I can see.

(COMPANY dances. Scene shifts.)

HOUSEKEEPER 1. Ay Mija como te estaba diciendo, esta señora Schwartzberg me esta volviendo loca. Ella me hace limpiar los pesos de rodilla.

HOUSEKEEPER 2. Por lo meños no te anda persiguiendo y vijilando ilando todo tus movimientos como mi jefa.

HOUSEKEEPER 1. Pues, mi jefa me hace subir una escalerita y limpiar los rincones del techo. Asi y asi … Que cingada es eso?

HOUSEKEEPER 2. Ay! Dios mio!

HOUSEKEEPER 1. Estos gringos salen con cada cosa. Vamonos!

(COMPANY dances, exits.)

LARRY. *(Alone onstage.)* I did it.

Scene 8

LARRY. *(On phone.)* What do you mean the FAA wants to sue me for five thousand dollars, Lenny? I don't have five thousand dollars. Because I spent every penny on the flight, that's why. Lenny, you have to appeal to the judge. Tell him about some of my ideas for the future, like people going to the grocery store with balloons and propeller packs or lifting people out of wheelchairs. Hold on, Lenny.

CAROL. *(Enters.)* Hey, guess what?

LARRY. Lenny, I got to go.

CAROL. You know what? I couldn't even get out of the garage. Every single news station was planted right in front of the house.

LARRY. Let's order.

CAROL. It was so amazing.

LARRY. Two Cokes, please.

CAROL. Did you see Channel 2?

LARRY and CAROL. Bill Baxx!

CAROL. They had the most amazing shot with the fire truck, all the balloons were hanging off. It looked so cool.

LARRY. Carol ... David Letterman called.

CAROL No!

LARRY. I'm going this weekend. They're putting me up at the Essex House.

CAROL. What about the Timex shoot?

LARRY. That's the great thing. They arranged everything with the Timex people. I'm going to do the Timex shoot and be on David Letterman. And Carol, David Letterman is sending me two first-class tickets to New York City. Do you copy?

CAROL. Yes, I copy. Oh my God, we're going to New York. I've never been to New York before. I'm so excited.

LARRY. I'm kind of worried about something though.

CAROL. What's the matter?

LARRY. Well, I have a space between my front teeth.

CAROL. Yeah?

LARRY. So does Dave. *(Pause.)* Do you think that's a problem? Do you think I should try to hide it somehow? Shove something up there, or caulk it. I just don't want to compete with Dave. You compete with Dave he gets bitter. He gets bitter, he gets angry. He gets angry, he gets mean. What do you think?

CAROL. Your teeth have nothing to do with why you're going on that show. You should just go out there and be yourself. Why don't you bring it up as a conversation piece or something, or just make a little joke of it.

TERRY. *(Enters.)* Excuse me.

LARRY. That's a good idea.

TERRY. Aren't you Larry Walters?

LARRY. Uh, yes. Yes, I am.

TERRY. Terry Hornsby. Doc Rausch's chemistry class. Remember me?

LARRY and CAROL. Oh, hey, Terry.

LARRY. How you doin' man?

TERRY. Great. Oh, hey, Carol. Say, that was some stunt you pulled the other day. I was watching the game with McKracken and Vichy, and we saw you on the news, man. I mean you did some wild stuff in high school, but that was a titan.

LARRY. Really? Well ....

TERRY. We were in hysterics for hours. I laughed so hard, I cried.

LARRY. Hey, Terry, bet you never thought you'd see me at

16,000 feet?

CAROL. Your hair's gotten long since high school, Terry.

TERRY. Dude, I got a chair of surf shops, so it kind of fits the image.

CAROL. Yeah, well I got to talk to Larry about some stuff. It's really good to see you.

TERRY. Well, great to see you guys. We were sure you'd be in jail at least a year on that thing.

(TERRY exits.)

LARRY. *(Shouting after TERRY.)* Oh, no. Hey, Terry, don't you worry about that FAA thing. I got lawyers working on that. You know if the Wright Brothers had to worry about the FAA, they would have never gotten off the ground at Kitty Hawk.

Scene 9

STEWARDESS. *(Overlaps following dialogue.)* Once again, ladies and gentlemen, we'd like to welcome you to Pan Am Flight 1069 to New York. Please extinguish all cigarettes and take a moment to check that all your carry-on baggage is stowed in the overhead compartment or under the seat in front of you. In case of emergency the four exits are marked with red and white signs, if we should experience a change in cabin pressure at any point during the flight, oxygen masks will drop down in front of you. Please secure your own mask before helping others, and should it become necessary, your seat cushion may be used as a flotation device. All safety information is outlined in the safety card located in the back pocket of the seat in front of you. Kindly restrict smoking to designated areas.

(LARRY enters with child-size lawn chair.)

STEWARDESS. Please fasten your seat belts as we prepare for take-off.

CAROL. Oh here he is.

STEWARDESS 1. Sir, that is not going to fit in the overhead compartment.

LARRY. Well it's going to fit somewhere because I measured it.

CAROL. He says he measured it.

STEWARDESS 1. Sir, would you like me to check it in the belly of the plane?

LARRY. You know we were promised first-class seats, and I know there must be room up there. I've heard musicians keep their instruments on the seats next to them.

STEWARDESS 1. Sir, even Eric Clapton surrendered his guitar. Let me just take this up front for you.

CAROL. Well, can you see if it'll just fit in the coat rack?

STEWARDESS 1. I'll try.

LARRY. I want to see where you're putting it.

(LARRY and ATTENDANT exit. LARRY re-enters.)

CAROL. Is it ok?

LARRY. I don't know. She just took it.

(LARRY rings for STEWARDESS.)

BELINDA. *(Enters.)* Yes, sir, how can I help you?

LARRY. Excuse me, I didn't get one of those cards that explains the emergency features of the craft.

BELINDA. Here you go, sir.

LARRY. Thank you.

LARRY. I'm particularly interested in the oxygen masks. I have some experience with high altitudes.

BELINDA. Enjoy your flight.

(BELINDA exits as STEWARDESS 1 enters.)

STEWARDESS 1. May I offer you a beverage?
CAROL. I'll have a tea with milk and one ....
LARRY. Do you have blender drinks?
STEWARDESS 1. Sir, we have beer, wine, sodas, various scotches.
LARRY. I'll have a Coke.
STEWARDESS 1. Complimentary nuts?
CAROL. Oh, that would be great.
LARRY. Oh, yes, please.

(STEWARDESS 1 throws the nuts and exits.)

LARRY. Carol, come here I want to show you something. You see how small that car is down there?
CAROL. Yeah?
LARRY. That's the way they look at 16,000 feet.
CAROL. Wow. That's what it looks like?
LARRY. Yeah. I could see so much more if what wing weren't there.
CAROL. Oh no.
LARRY. Let me handle this.

(LARRY rings for STEWARDESS.)

BELINDA. *(Enters.)* Yes sir, how can I help you?
LARRY. I'm sorry to bother you, but I'm flying to New York to be on David Letterman and the producers promised us first-class seats and I noticed when I was up there before that there were some empty seats and I was wondering if we might be able to move up there since we're suppose to be there anyway?
BELINDA. I'm sorry sir, I'm afraid I'm not authorized to upgrade you, but if you don't mind my asking what will you be doing on David Letterman?

LARRY. I'm the lawn chair pilot.

BELINDA. Oh, my God! You are the guy with the balloons and the lawn chair. Right? I thought I recognized you from somewhere. I read about you in all the papers. Larry Walters, right?

LARRY. You got it.

BELINDA. Belinda. Belinda DiAngelo.

LARRY. Hi, I'm Larry—Larry Walters.

BELINDA. Oh my God, this is such an honor to meet you. You don't know, it really is, you know. What you did up there at 16,000 feet was so inspiring!

LARRY. Oh, thank you.

BELINDA. No. Thank you.

CAROL. Oh, I'm Carol.

BELINDA. Hi, Carol.

CAROL. Hi.

BELINDA. Is that the chair that you used in the flight?

LARRY and CAROL. No—

LARRY. I'm taking that for David Letterman. The actual chair I gave away to some kids who helped me out of the power lines.

CAROL. Yeah, we sure regret that.

LARRY. It belongs in the Smithsonian with a diorama and me ....

BELINDA. That's so generous of you. You know, to give to the little people in that way.

CAROL. It's not really about the little people.

LARRY. It's about history.

CAROL. Yeah, it's about history.

BELINDA. Oh, yeah, yeah.

LARRY. Are you from New York?

BELINDA. How could you tell?

LARRY. It's in your eyes.

BELINDA. So, you're going to get a chance to see the sights while you're in the Big Apple?

CAROL. Well, we don't really have a whole lot of time. But we're definitely going to the Empire State Building, the Statue of

Liberty, Central Park and Coney Island—

LARRY. Hot dogs!

CAROL. Yeah, we want to try those hot dogs!

BELINDA. I don't know if you want to go all the way out to Brooklyn, I gotta tell you it's a real schlep.

LARRY. Let's cross that off our list. It sounds like a "schlep." What would you recommend?

BELINDA. Oh definitely Studio 54. A celeb like you could get in like this.

(BELINDA snaps her fingers.)

LARRY. *(Sings. BELINDA joins in.)* "Stayin' alive, stayin' alive." Did you always want to be a stewardess? I mean did you ever think about being a pilot or flying?

BELINDA. Actually, I always wanted to be a Rockette. You know, like in Radio City. But I didn't meet the height requirement.

CAROL. I know what that feels like because I had an experience like that—

LARRY. Carol, Carol. I think flying's a lot like dancing. Rockette, rocket.

CAROL. Are the restrooms in the back of the plane?

BELINDA. Straight back, honey. You can't miss it.

(CAROL exits.)

BELINDA. So did you always want to fly in a lawn chair?

LARRY. When I was eight years old my dad took me to Disneyland and one of the first things I saw when I got there was this guy—

BELINDA. Pluto?

LARRY. He was holding this big bouquet of balloons. And my dad bought me one of the balloons and I took it home and I spent the whole day attaching toys to it trying to get the balloon to lift the toy.

And I finally got it to lift this one toy, and it just hovered, just floated across the room. And that's when I knew I wanted to float in a balloon.

BELINDA. That is one of the most beautiful stories I have ever heard. You know that story belongs in a movie. Have you ever thought about making your story into a movie of the week or somethin'?

LARRY. Have you ever seen *Somewhere in Time?*

BELINDA. No.

LARRY. Oh it's great! It's got Christopher Reeve!

(CAROL enters.)

BELINDA. *Superman,* right?

LARRY. Right, but he's very different in this movie, Belinda. He's very serious.

CAROL. Oh, *Somewhere in Time?* Larry and I love that movie.

BELINDA. No. No. Larry Walters does not belong in coach. I'm going to see what I can do about this first-class situation. *(Exits. Pause. Re-enters.)* Hello again.

LARRY and CAROL. Hi.

BELINDA. I thought you might want another. *(Gives LARRY a Coke.)* Oh, by the way, I was able to secure seating in first class.

CAROL. Oh super!

LARRY. Great!

BELINDA. Unfortunately, I could only allocate one seat.

CAROL. Well that's okay.

BELINDA. Well maybe one of your would like to go up there?

CAROL. No, that's okay.

BELINDA. Okay, well if you change your mind or if you need anything else you just give me a buzz.

CAROL. Okay.

LARRY. Okay.

CAROL. Thank you.

BELINDA. You're welcome

(BELINDA exits.)

LARRY. Maybe one of us should go up there.
CAROL. Would you really want to do that?
LARRY. They promised us first-class seats. One of us should be able to go up there and stretch out.
CAROL. No. We should stick together.
LARRY. Now I'm worried about that chair. What if someone recognizes me, they see the chair, they put two and two together, and they take it?
CAROL. Larry, we're on a plane. Where are they gonna go?
LARRY. Would you check on it for me? Please?
CAROL. Okay. I'll go check on your chair. I'll be right back.

(CAROL exits. Pause. LARRY rings for STEWARDESS.)

BELINDA. Larry.
LARRY. I was wondering, do you think I could try out first class? Just for a couple of minutes.
BELINDA. Oh yeah, for as long as you want.
LARRY. Great.

(LARRY and BELINDA exit.)

Scene 10

LARRY. Wow, this is great!
KIMBA. Hi I'm Kimba. I'm your hair and makeup artist. This is Nicholas, Sandy Shiner's assistant.
LARRY. Is that food for me because I'm starving?

KIMBA. Nicholas, love, make him up a plate. I need to operate on my patient.

NICHOLAS. Something to drink?

LARRY. Well, a Coke would be great.

KIMBA. Oh, wow you've got really tough hair. I'm going to have to wet you.

LARRY. Nick, I was wondering, am I going to be wearing the Explorer One or the Explorer Two watch? The Explorer Two is so much beefier ...

KIMBA. Please look forward.

LARRY. ... and it would show up better in the shoot.

NICHOLAS. I just need to get your signature on a couple of things while Kimba works her magic.

KIMBA. He's got no eyes, eyes like two dead fish. Sunglasses, great!

LARRY. No, actually I didn't wear sunglasses during the flight. I wore aviators. You know, Nick, you might be interested in this. When Inspiration One first took off there was a sudden gust wind and my aviators fell off. But luckily I had another pair.

NICHOLAS. Great and one more right here.

LARRY. And I think that might be something we want to put in the shoot. I really do, Nick.

KIMBA. Nicholas, this hair is a travesty. I'm going to have to hat him.

(KIMBA tries a series of hats on LARRY.)

LARRY. No, see I didn't wear a hat during the flight ....

KIMBA. Nick, Nick, darling what do you think?

NICHOLAS. Hmm, too Gilligan.

LARRY. No, see I didn't wear a hat during the flight.

NICHOLAS. Perfect.

KIMBA. I'll just take a little shine off of you and then I'm done.

LARRY. Look, I didn't wear a hat during the flight or

sunglasses! Nick, I just want it to be authentic.

NICHOLAS. Look, Larry, we don't have to do the shoot if you don't want to. Okay, Kimba, who's next?

KIMBA. Mike Wallace. Tick, Tick, Tick ....

LARRY. Okay, Nick, that hat's great.

NICHOLAS. Fine, follow me, please.

(NICK exits.)

KIMBA. Are you really the lawn chair guy?

LARRY. You must have seen my picture in *The New York Times*?

KIMBA. I only read the *Post*.

Scene 11

LARRY. *(On phone, holding miniature lawn chair.)* No, George, I just don't want you to run the story. It's my story, George. No, it's not your writing. I like it. I'm halfway through *Paper Lion* right now. I've got a lot of irons in the fire ....

BRECKY. *(Entering.)* Larry ... Larry ... Larry. Okay. Saul Bellow's caught in traffic, so we're going to bump you up.

LARRY. George, I gotta go. I've been bumped.

BRECKY. You're going on right after Teri Garr. Check your fly. Just kidding. Relax. You have two whole minutes. She's such a talker. What's this?

LARRY. Well, this is a model I brought for Dave.

BRECKY. I love it. Okay, Larry, focus. There will be three cameras. Camera one, two, three. I'll be behind camera one. If the ping pong balls fall down during the interview, don't pay any attention. Dave's going to announce you, Paul's going to play *Up, Up, and Away*, the monkey cam's going to follow you in, and you're going to sit in the chair.

LARRY. If you can imagine, the balloons were up here—

BRECKY. Larry, Larry, Dave is going to love this, and if he loves this he's going to love you. Okay?

LARRY. Okay.

BRECKY. Okay, great. So, why a lawn chair?

LARRY. Well in Vietnam—

BRECKY. Make it short.

LARRY. Well, they're very comfortable—

BRECKY. What's next on the agenda? Book deal, movie deal?

LARRY. Book deal, movie deal ....

BRECKY. Okay, Mike, thirty seconds. Okay, Larry. Places.

(LARRY enters into spotlight with child-size lawn chair. He sits in it. Audience roars with laughter.)

Scene 12

LARRY. *(At podium.)* The sky has no limits. There are no limits. I achieved my dream. You can achieve yours. Imagine being tethered to truck and that tether suddenly snaps and you shoot up to 16,000 feet. But by the grace of God I did it, and if I can do it you can do it. You, the Chamber of Commerce here in Lolita, California. Thank you. Thank you. I've been on the road for six weeks. It's wonderful to be here doing these motivational seminars. But I'm doing these just for the time being, because I have other plans for the future. Is everybody motivated?

(Scene shifts.)

FAN 1. We'll have a lawn chair party. Everyone will bring a lawn chair. Maybe balloons.

FAN 2. What will we charge?

FAN 1. Twenty-five dollars. Five dollars will go to the defense fund.

FAN 2. What's the rest for?

FAN 1. Beer.

(Scene shifts.)

LARRY. *(At podium.)* Remember you're never too young to have a dream. Thank you. Thank you. It's wonderful to be here in Heath Cliffs addressing the Young Astronomers. I've been on the road now for about seven months. Now kids, you can never be prepared for what's going to happen when you're flying in a lawn chair. There're all sorts of variables. Like wind drift. Now, kids, there are some things you just have to leave to ….

(Scene shifts.)

PARK RANGER 1. Is that park ranger job still available?

PARK RANGER 2. Why?

PARK RANGER 1. That lawn chair guy, he wants it.

PARK RANGER 2. The lawn chair guy?

PARK RANGER 1. We can stick him with the volunteers.

(Scene shifts.)

LARRY. *(At podium.)* No I'm not going to be able to make it for Thanksgiving, Carol. I really just want to be on my own right now. No, no the motivational seminars are going great. No, no tell your mom thanks. I'm not going to be able to make it for Christmas either. I got that job with the forest service so I think I'm going to do a lot of hiking and camping and thinking, because I've been doing a lot of thinking. About heaven. Do you remember in *Somewhere in Time* at the end of the movie when they're just standing there … you gotta go? Carol, I'll always think of you as my girlfriend—Carol? Carol?

(Scene shifts.)

LARRY. *(At podium.)* The sky has no limits, there are no limits. I achieved my dream. You can achieve yours. Imagine being tethered to a truck and that tether snaps and you shoot up to 16,000 feet. But by the grace of God I did it. And if I can do it, you certainly can do it. You, the House of Pilgrims here in San Cristo Cristo, California.
ELIAHU. I for one was personally moved by your story.
LAGRIMA. And I too.
COMFORT. Thank you brother Eliahu, Sister Lagrima. I too was personally moved by your journey. *(SISTER HUSH clears her throat.)* So was Sister Hush. My name is Sister Comfort Finnhagen, and I would like to welcome you to the House of Pilgrims.
LARRY. Why were you all so affected?
ELIAHU. Just as the bird of peace descended from on high to anoint the chosen one, so too have you descended with your apparatus from the heavens bringing your message to our multitudes.
LARRY. It's just a lawn chair.
ELIAHU. But you were in the lawn chair.
LARRY. Well, I was the pilot.
COMFORT. I think you must be higher that 16,000 feet now, Larry. I see blue skies. Yes? Yes?
LARRY. I'm feeling something. I'm just not sure what it is.
LAGRIMA. The ways of our creator are a mystery to us all Brother Larry.
LARRY. Did you see *Somewhere in Time*? At the end of the movie they're standing on this cloud … it looked just like … it looked just like ….
ELIAHU. This brings to mind the story of the mustard seed. Though small as a grain of sand, the mustard seed once sewn upon the fertile soil grows great and mighty roots, a powerful trunk, bears fruit and shade for us all. Yea, thought the spirit is willing the flesh is

weak. There is no way to peace, Brother Walters. Peace is simply the way.

ALL. *(Singing.)*
Grinding corn, grinding corn
You and I grinding corn
Red and green and yellow
You and I are grinding corn.

LARRY. The wise men came home another way.

Scene 13

LARRY. Margaret? Margaret? It's me, Larry.
MOM. Oh Larry? Sweetie, what time is it?
LARRY. It's 9:30.
MOM. Oh Lar, dinner was for 6:30. Carol's already gone.
LARRY. I missed everybody.
MOM. We had nachos and sangria.
LARRY. I wanted to tell everybody ....
MOM. Oh Lar, did you see the pictures in the dining area? There's the one of you and Carol in the jeep and that one of you when you got tangled in the power lines.
LARRY. You took down the Last Supper?
MOM. It's been ten years.
LARRY. Ten years.
MOM. Lar, why'd you do it?
LARRY. A man just can't sit around.
MOM. Were you scared?
LARRY. Margaret, I was holding onto that chair. I was just clutching it. I couldn't see anything. I came through the clouds. And it was clear. I could see everything. It was blue. Just blue, blue sky.
MOM. And then you had to come down. Kind of like waking up,

huh?

LARRY. Margaret, will you sing that hymn?

MOM. Oh, sweetie.

LARRY. The one you always used to play.

MOM. Oh. Lar did you hear about Pretty Girl? She crawled into the oven and just died. When Carol pulled her out she felt just like a little kitten. *(Singing.)* The Lord's my Shepard, I'll not want. He maketh me to lie.

MOM and LARRY. *(Singing.)* In pastures green He leadeth me, the quiet waters by.

MOM. *(Singing.)* He leadeth me. He leadeth me, the quiet waters by. Lar? *(He touches her.)* Oh, sweetie, I'd thought you'd gone. There's food in the fridge. Lar? Lar?

Scene 14

(Voice over from top of play continues.)

VOICEOVER. Walters subsequently fell on hard times, became bankrupt, and died by his own hand in 1993. But his memory survives as a model of those qualities of independence, vision, and disregard for common caution without which aviation would never have come into being.

(LARRY flies in the lawn chair.)

END OF PLAY

SKIN DEEP
Jon Lonoff

Comedy / 2m, 2f / Interior Unit Set

In *Skin Deep*, a large, lovable, lonely-heart, named Maureen Mulligan, gives romance one last shot on a blind-date with sweet awkward Joseph Spinelli; she's learned to pepper her speech with jokes to hide insecurities about her weight and appearance, while he's almost dangerously forthright, saying everything that comes to his mind. They both know they're perfect for each other, and in time they come to admit it.

They were set up on the date by Maureen's sister Sheila and her husband Squire, who are having problems of their own: Sheila undergoes a non-stop series of cosmetic surgeries to hang onto the attractive and much-desired Squire, who may or may not have long ago held designs on Maureen, who introduced him to Sheila. With Maureen particularly vulnerable to both hurting and being hurt, the time is ripe for all these unspoken issues to bubble to the surface.

"Warm-hearted comedy … the laughter was literally show-stopping. A winning play, with enough good-humored laughs and sentiment to keep you smiling from beginning to end."
- TalkinBroadway.com

"It's a little Paddy Chayefsky, a lot Neil Simon and a quick-witted, intelligent voyage into the not-so-tranquil seas of middle-aged love and dating. The dialogue is crackling and hilarious; the plot simple but well-turned; the characters endearing and quirky; and lurking beneath the merriment is so much heartache that you'll stand up and cheer when the unlikely couple makes it to the inevitable final clinch."
- NYTheatreWorld.Com

COCKEYED
William Missouri Downs

Comedy / 3m, 1f / Unit Set

Phil, an average nice guy, is madly in love with the beautiful Sophia. The only problem is that she's unaware of his existence. He tries to introduce himself but she looks right through him. When Phil discovers Sophia has a glass eye, he thinks that might be the problem, but soon realizes that she really can't see him. Perhaps he is caught in a philosophical hyperspace or dualistic reality or perhaps beautiful women are just unaware of nice guys. Armed only with a B.A. in philosophy, Phil sets out to prove his existence and win Sophia's heart. This fast moving farce is the winner of the HotCity Theatre's GreenHouse New Play Festival. The St. Louis Post-Dispatch called Cockeyed a clever romantic comedy, Talkin' Broadway called it "hilarious," while Playback Magazine said that it was "fresh and invigorating."

Winner!
of the HotCity Theatre GreenHouse New Play Festival

"Rocking with laughter...hilarious...polished and engaging
work draws heavily on the age-old conventions of farce:
improbable situations, exaggerated characters, amazing
coincidences, absurd misunderstandings, people hiding
in closets and barely missing each other as they run in and
out of doors...full of comic momentum as Cockeyed hurtles
toward its conclusion."
- Talkin' Broadway

THE OFFICE PLAYS
Two full length plays by Adam Bock

THE RECEPTIONIST
Comedy / 2m, 2f / Interior

At the start of a typical day in the Northeast Office, Beverly deals effortlessly with ringing phones and her colleague's romantic troubles. But the appearance of a charming rep from the Central Office disrupts the friendly routine. And as the true nature of the company's business becomes apparent, The Receptionist raises disquieting, provocative questions about the consequences of complicity with evil.

"...Mr. Bock's poisoned Post-it note of a play."
- New York Times

"Bock's intense initial focus on the routine goes to the heart of
The Receptionist's pointed, painfully timely allegory... elliptical,
provocative play..."
- Time Out New York

THE THUGS
Comedy / 2m, 6f / Interior

The Obie Award winning dark comedy about work, thunder and the mysterious things that are happening on the 9th floor of a big law firm. When a group of temps try to discover the secrets that lurk in the hidden crevices of their workplace, they realize they would rather believe in gossip and rumors than face dangerous realities.

"Bock starts you off giggling, but leaves you with a chill."
- Time Out New York

"... a delightfully paranoid little nightmare that is both more
chillingly realistic and pointedly absurd than anything
John Grisham ever dreamed up."
- New York Times

www.ingramcontent.com/pod-product-compliance
Lightning Source LLC
Chambersburg PA
CBHW070420120726
47909CB00005B/1729